Kabbit's Nap

Rabbit's feeling sleepy.
She curls up in a chair.

Tap! Tap! Who's that?
Oh dear! It's Builder Bear.

Where can Rabbit have her nap?
The window seat looks nice.

Bang! Clash! Who's that?
Oh no! A band of mice.

Rabbit's in her deckchair.
A doze would be so good.

Whack! Crack! Who's that?
It's Fox – he's chopping wood.

"A shady tree!" says Rabbit.
"The kind of spot I like."

Ting-a-ling! Who's that?
It's Tortoise on his bike.

Poor tired Rabbit goes back home.
She yawns and rubs her eyes.

Rat-a-tat! Who's that?
"Your friends with a surprise!"

"Hush-a-bunny! Tra-la-la!
We'll sing you off to sleep!"

Zzzzz! Zzzzz! What's that?
Shall we have a peep?

Fox's
Socks

Poor old Fox
Has lost his socks.

He looks in a chest,
And finds his vest.

On it goes.
"But I've got cold toes!"

Under the stair
Is a shirt to wear.

The shirt goes on.
"But my socks! They've gone!"

In a cupboard up high,
He finds his bow tie.

The tie looks neat.
"But I've got bare feet!"

Under the mat
He finds his hat.

"But where are my socks?"
Says poor old Fox.

He looks in the clock,
And finds one sock!

But Fox needs two.
What can he do?

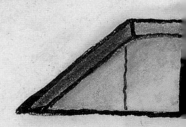

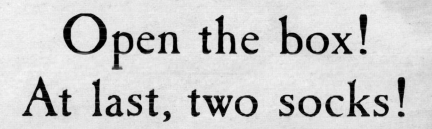

Open the box!
At last, two socks!

First published 2000 by Campbell Books
This edition published 2015 by Macmillan Children's Books
a division of Macmillan Publishers Limited
20 New Wharf Road, London N1 9RR
Basingstoke and Oxford
Associated companies throughout the world
www.panmacmillan.com

ISBN: 978-1-4472-7345-5

1 3 5 7 9 8 6 4 2

A CIP catalogue record for this book is available from the British Library.

Printed in Malaysia